This boo belongs to:

. . . .

To Grandad.

www.dk.com

First published in Great Britain in 1999
by Dorling Kindersley Limited,
9 Henrietta Street, London WC2E 8PS

2 4 6 8 10 9 7 5 3 1

A CIP catalogue record for this book is available from the British Library.

ISBN 0-7513-7431-8 (Hardback)
ISBN 0-7513-6245-X (Paperback)

Colour reproduction by Dot Gradations, UK
Printed in Hong Kong by Wing King Tong

What About Me?

By Helen
Stephens

Charlie and his friends

were playing...

...when katy said, "Look, this is Arthur. He's new and he needs some friends."

All Charlie's friends went to play with Arthur.

"But you were playing with me!"
cried Charlie. "What about me?"

Charlie wondered how he could get his friends to play with him instead of Arthur.

"Look, everybody!" said Charlie.

"It's much more fun over here. Why don't you play with me?"

"Why won't you play, Charlie?"
said Katy.

"Because everyone wants to play with Arthur now. What about me?"

"Arthur is new and he needs some friends," said Katy.

"Look, he needs a special friend to help him ride your scooter."

said Charlie. "Climb on!"

They all joined in...

and Charlie thought how nice it

was to play with everyone.
Especially Arthur.